Ghostly Tales

AND MYSTERIOUS HAPPENINGS OF OLD MONTEREY...*and Beyond*

Randall A. Reinstedt

Illustrated by

Ed Greco and Tony Hrusa

Ghost Town Publications
Carmel, California
www.ghosttownpub.com

For other books by Randall A. Reinstedt, see page 73. If bookstores in your area do not carry these titles, copies may be ordered by writing to . . .

Ghost Town Publications
P.O. Drawer 5998
Carmel, CA 93921

Or visit our web site:

www.ghosttownpub.com

10 9 8 7 6 5 4 3 2 1

Manufactured in the United States of America

ISBN 978-0-933818-04-0

Library of Congress Control Number: 2007907617

For the story illustrated on the cover, see "A human skull stared at him through eyeless holes . . ." on page 38.

Edited by John Bergez
Typesetting by Erick and Mary Ann Reinstedt

*This book is dedicated to the
old-timers—and to all those who take
the time to record their stories*

Contents

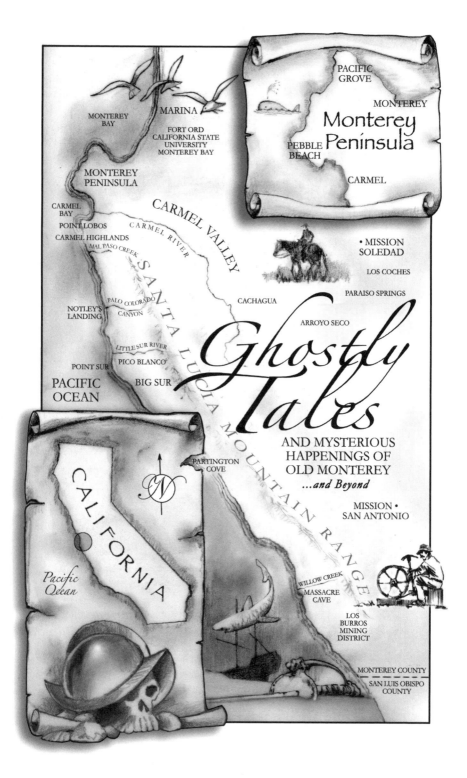

PACIFIC
GROVE

MONTEREY

Monterey
Peninsula

PEBBLE
BEACH

CARMEL

MONTEREY
BAY

MARINA

FORT ORD
CALIFORNIA STATE
UNIVERSITY
MONTEREY BAY

MONTEREY
PENINSULA

CARMEL VALLEY

CARMEL
BAY

POINT LOBOS

CARMEL HIGHLANDS

MAL PASO CREEK

CARMEL RIVER

• MISSION
SOLEDAD

LOS COCHES

PARAISO SPRINGS

PALO COLORADO
CANYON

NOTLEY'S
LANDING

CACHAGUA

ARROYO SECO

LITTLE SUR RIVER

PICO BLANCO

POINT SUR

PACIFIC
OCEAN

BIG SUR

SANTA LUCIA MOUNTAIN RANGE

Ghostly Tales

AND MYSTERIOUS
HAPPENINGS OF
OLD MONTEREY
...and Beyond

PARTINGTON
COVE

N

CALIFORNIA

MISSION •
SAN ANTONIO

*Pacific
Ocean*

WILLOW CREEK

MASSACRE
CAVE

LOS
BURROS
MINING
DISTRICT

MONTEREY COUNTY

SAN LUIS OBISPO
COUNTY

Author's Note

When first visiting Monterey, California's original capital city, visitors are delighted, and sometimes amazed, by the number of historic buildings that are found throughout the town. If they are at all interested in history, they thrill to the events that took place in the picturesque structures, and they are impressed by the way the buildings have been preserved. In looking into the varied background of these aged adobes, and in learning that many of them date back to the early to mid 1800s, most show little surprise when they learn that many of the structures also boast a history of ghosts and mysterious happenings. This "haunted history" of old Monterey—together with its beautiful peninsula and selected other sections of Monterey County—is the subject of this volume.

There are a few points I should explain at the outset. This book was originally published in 1977 as *Ghostly Tales and Mysterious Happenings of Old Monterey.* It is now thirty years later, and I thought it was time to polish it up, tweak a few of the tales, add a new cover, create titles for the stories, incorporate some new art, and enlarge the type size (good grief, the older I got, the harder it was to read!). Apart from these changes, the book remains much the same. However, I should mention that I did delete one tale that appeared in the first edition, as new facts came to light discounting much of the information regarding that story.

The original edition of this book followed the publication of my first "ghost book," *Ghosts, Bandits and Legends of Old Monterey, Carmel and Surrounding Areas,* which told many of the better-known ghost stories connected with a number of historic structures, including such famous locations as the Robert

1

Louis Stevenson House and the Royal Presidio Chapel and its old rectory. In an effort not to duplicate any of these accounts, many of these buildings are not mentioned in this text. Where the same structures are included in both publications, it is because additional stories involving the buildings came to light after my first book was published.

With these preliminaries taken care of, it is time to begin our journey. Whether you are new to this book, or revisiting it in its new incarnation, I hope you will enjoy your excursion into the spooky side of the history of old Monterey—and beyond.

Randall A. Reinstedt

Ghostly Tales and Mysterious Happenings of Old Monterey . . . and Beyond

California's Number One State Historical Monument . . .

One of old Monterey's most historic structures is known to history buffs as California's Number One State Historical Monument. Among locals, it is better known as the Custom House. Situated near the entrance of Monterey's famed Fisherman's Wharf, the Custom House boasts a long history of ghostly happenings since construction began on the structure in the 1820s. Other than eerie feelings and a haunted tower, accounts about the aged adobe tell of concealed graves, hidden treasure, and the ghosts of several long-dead Montereyans.

Many believe that tales of ghosts began with a variety of renters who occupied the structure in the late 1800s, long after the building served as a Custom House. Perhaps the best known of these stories was shared by a family of five, consisting of a man, three women, and a very young child. Among the odd occurrences reportedly experienced by the family were a black cat that appeared and disappeared at will, coughing and assorted other sounds heard in unoccupied rooms, and deafening swooshing and rattling sounds coming from the walls. Stranger still was the discovery of the infant—who was too young to crawl or pull himself from his basket—asleep in a bed of ashes across the room from where he had been left.

As if all this wasn't enough, the frightened family was also visited in the dead of night by a variety of long-departed and obviously troubled souls. On a number of occasions one woman in particular was "spooked" by nighttime visits from the spirit of a long-dead man of Mexican descent and a young lad who was always by his side. During each of the first three visits, the man told how he had been killed—along with the boy—for the gold he had hidden in the adobe. Describing how he and his young friend had been buried at the foot of the stairs leading to "the tower," the man pleaded with the woman to find the graves and give the bodies a proper burial in the Catholic cemetery.*

With the family being quite shaken, and with the graves remaining unfound, the woman was again visited in the night. During this fourth visitation, however, she was confronted by a skeleton possessing the voice of the deceased Mexican. As the trembling woman watched—and perhaps murmured a hasty prayer or two—the bony apparition pointed to the corner of the upstairs room and spoke of the hidden gold. Looking in the direction the skeleton was pointing, the terrified woman saw what appeared to be an aged metal container with an abundance of gold coins spilling from its top. As she stared in awe, both the skeleton and the gold slowly faded from sight.

The following morning, upon discussing the mysterious circumstances of the night before, the family became intrigued with the thought of gold being hidden in the building. However, several hours of prying up floorboards and looking in various nooks and crannies failed to turn up any sign of treasure—or graves.

---

*Interestingly, the Custom House today has two towers—in reality, they are second-story rooms, with interior staircases, located at each end of the building—but prior to the 1840s the structure is said to have had only one tower. Perhaps when the Mexican man and the boy were killed, there was only one upstairs room and staircase in the adobe.

Looking in the direction the skeleton was pointing, the terrified woman saw an aged metal container with an abundance of gold coins spilling from its top . . .

The family finally moved from the adobe after one particularly trying night when the man of the house, who slept in a downstairs room, was thrown from his bed—on three separate occasions—by unseen hands. Convinced that the adobe was inhabited by spirits of the dead, and that living mortals were unwanted intruders in the spirits' domicile, the man decided to take his family and seek safer shelter in a less crowded structure!

The ghostly figure of an aged fisherman . . .

While we're in the area of Fisherman's Wharf, I'd like to share the experience of a woman from our neighboring state of Nevada who was introduced to me as "an expert on ghosts and happenings of the supernatural." After visiting a number of Monterey's older buildings, the woman enthusiastically spoke of feeling the presence of ghosts and spirits in many of the community's historic structures.

Apart from vouching for the existence of ghosts in Monterey's adobes, the lady told of a personal encounter with a local spirit. While exploring Fisherman's Wharf during one early-morning stroll, she saw the ghostly figure of an aged fisherman sitting on the pier, staring out to sea. Feeling sorry for the lonely man, the lady approached the gaunt figure and asked if she could be of help. Hardly taking his eyes from the sea, the grizzled old fisherman replied gruffly that he was perfectly content as he was.

Strange happenings and odd sensations . . .

Only a few blocks from Monterey's waterfront is beautiful Colton Hall. The building was named after Walter Colton, the first American *alcalde* (mayor) of Monterey. Built by prisoners, and financed to a large extent by fines collected from gamblers and taxes on liquor shops, the two-story structure was completed in March of 1849. It was soon hailed as "the most elegant edifice" in all of California, and to this day it remains a showplace of old Monterey.

Apart from its splendid appearance, Colton Hall has the historic distinction of being the site of California's constitutional convention, which took place from early September through mid October in 1849. The stately structure also served as one of the area's first schools as well as a meeting place for the local citizenry.*

Like so many aged structures, Colton Hall has a history of mysterious happenings. From time to time various museum workers have told me about strange events and odd sensations they have experienced at the site. Perhaps, as some people believe, these occurrences are brought about by the spirits of prisoners who, in days gone by, were unceremoniously hanged from Colton Hall's porch! As numerous early tales tell us, with Monterey's old jail (circa 1854) adjoining the hall, the structure's balconied porch served as a handy scaffold on more than one occasion.

Colton Hall's last hanging is documented in an aged publication about long-ago happenings in Monterey. According to this account, even though the participants in what appears to be a Monterey-style vigilante committee showed little concern for the law, they did see fit to prevent the students of Colton Hall School from viewing the proceedings. With names purposely omitted, the account stated: "An Indian from the valley who had shot ——— was brought to speedy justice at the end of a rope by the rancher's friends in Monterey. It was recess time at Colton Hall school, and ——— insisted that Mrs. ———, the

---

*Today the building's second floor is set up as a museum, and appears much the way it did during the constitutional convention.

teacher, gather the youngsters inside the schoolroom to protect them from the gruesome scene."*

The whimpering sounds of a child crying . . .

Approximately one block southeast of Colton Hall is the well-preserved Stokes Adobe. Built in the 1830s and 40s, this attractive two-story structure has played a colorful part in Monterey's past. Upon its completion the building was considered one of the most imposing homes in the capital city, and it was here that many of old Monterey's *cascarone* balls—one of the town's most popular social events—were held. Today the Stokes Adobe still serves as one of the community's favorite gathering places, as it houses an award-winning restaurant.

Of interest to us here are tales of a variety of perplexing happenings that take place in the historic structure. Most of those who have experienced these events agree that they usually occur in the wee hours of the morning. Such inexplicable occurrences as the unmistakable sounds of someone walking through upstairs rooms after the building has been checked and no one is there, or the whimpering sounds of a child crying—again, after a complete check of the structure has been made—are enough to cause considerable concern among those who have experienced them. But perhaps the most unnerving, or at least frustrating, of all the happenings takes place when the last person to leave the building reaches the parking lot after having secured the structure for the night, only to have all the lights suddenly turn on, requiring an additional trip back

---

*Even though the source from which the quotation regarding the "last" Colton Hall hanging is respected by many, several local history buffs question the accuracy of the report. Perhaps I should add here that there is also some controversy about whether *anyone* was ever hanged from the Colton Hall porch.

to the building and yet another fruitless search through the now well-lit rooms.

Framed in the glow of the unearthly light . . .

Not far from the Stokes Adobe, and near the heart of old Monterey, was once a section of town where a number of Monterey's not-so-fortunate citizens lived. Down on their luck, and in some cases a bit more interested in the "good life" than an honest day's work, the people of this area were shunned by some and ignored by others.

Among the inhabitants of this neglected neighborhood was a quiet, peace-loving family who lived in a weathered board-and-bat shack. One of the children of this down-and-out family was a proud and pretty little girl who was a popular addition to the local parochial school. Suddenly, however, the young miss was absent from school for several days. After hearing rumors that her family had mysteriously left town, a group of the girl's friends decided to visit her house in hopes of finding out what had become of her. Gathering their nerve, as they had often been told not to venture into "that part" of town, the girls cautiously crept through a thick evening fog, eventually reaching the run-down shack that had been the girl's home.

After getting no response to their repeated knocks, the girls bravely decided to peek through one of the front windows. Tiptoeing to the nearest window, they peered through ragged curtains, only to find the house empty except for a strange glow on the opposite side of the room. Framed in the glow of the unearthly light was the face of their friend. She looked as if she were in a deep sleep.

Terrified by the eerie glow and the strange stillness of their friend, the girls ran from the shack as fast as they could. Only later did they learn that the girl they had gone to see had died in the house a few days before their visit!

Tiptoeing to the nearest window, they peered through ragged curtains, only to find the house empty except for a strange glow on the opposite side of the room . . .

Suddenly she felt a tightness in her throat . . .

Our next tale takes us from a ramshackle neighborhood to a very dignified and proper section of old Monterey, where a large home went up for sale not too many years ago. A certain woman became extremely interested in the property and was entrusted with the key by the real estate firm handling the sale. Told to visit the home at her convenience, the prospective buyer made several trips to the house, becoming more impressed with each visit.

Having almost decided to purchase the property, the lady decided she should make one last inspection before saying yes. It was during this final visit that she walked into a spacious downstairs bedroom and became absorbed with thoughts of how best to arrange her furniture. While she was standing in the center of the room, engrossed in her thoughts, the door to the bedroom suddenly slammed shut. Startled by the noise, the woman immediately started toward the door. Suddenly, however, she felt a tightness in her throat and had great difficulty breathing. Frightened by what was taking place, the woman struggled to reach the door, only to find she could barely budge it. Finally, with the tightness in her throat becoming almost unbearable, she managed to force the door open and run from the room. As soon as she was free of the bedroom, the tightness in her throat disappeared, and she could breathe normally again.

Not surprisingly, after this experience the lady was convinced that the house wasn't for her. Returning the key to the real estate people, she told them about the terrifying incident. Nodding as if they had heard similar tales before, they proceeded to tell her that other visitors had also had a number of odd and frightening experiences while in the bedroom. In finishing their story, the real estate people confessed that upon checking into the history of the house, they had learned that a woman had once been strangled in that very room!

"The Most Elegant Seaside Establishment in the World" . . .

Long noted for its history and its importance as the site of California's first capital city, the Monterey Peninsula is also renowned as a playground for the rich and a gathering place for the famous. This aspect of the Peninsula's fame dates back at least as far as the opening of the fabulous Hotel Del Monte in 1880. Advertised as The Most Elegant Seaside Establishment in the World, the "Del Monte" more than lived up to its billing as it played host to countless internationally known personalities, including royalty, maharajas, diplomats, and U.S. presidents.

Today the former hotel, and its spacious grounds, are the property of the United States government. Known as the Naval Postgraduate School, the facility has also often been called "the Annapolis of the West." Even though the old buildings no longer host visiting royalty or globe-trotting maharajas, many of the stories connected with the elegant structures are still very much a part of the history of Monterey.

A surprising number of these tales involve the supernatural, or at least the paranormal. Over the years many ghostly and mysterious happenings are reported to have occurred in various parts of the hotel complex. The majority of the stories describe events that are said to have taken place in the elaborate main building, known today as Herrmann Hall. This imposing structure rose from the ashes of two disastrous fires (circa 1887 and 1924). Surrounded by beautiful gardens, it boasts a striking roof of red tile, a Spanish-style tower that rises 120 feet in the air, a dining hall that stretches to 200 feet in length, and—according to a number of workers—secret corridors that ramble about within its walls.

One report concerning Herrmann Hall, which was shared with me by the kitchen employee who experienced the event, takes us back to the American bicentennial year of 1976. As the witness described it, he happened to look up from his duties one evening when he noticed the figure of a middle-aged gentleman, attired in a suit of gray and sporting a neatly trimmed beard, seated all alone at a large banquet table in the upstairs ballroom. The distinguished-looking gentleman was staring at the worker "as if he was angry and impatient to be served." This

The distinguished-looking gentleman was staring at the worker "as if he was angry and impatient to be served . . ."

may not sound terribly mysterious until one realizes that in dress and appearance the impatient visitor exactly matched the description of the famed "Man in Gray" (the building's best-known ghost) and, moreover, that the figure had apparently materialized out of thin air! Not lingering to inquire what the spectral gentleman wanted, the employee exited the room on the run, stopping only when he reached the safety of the kitchen and his fellow workers.

It took several minutes for the shaken worker to regain his composure. Only then did the members of the kitchen staff learn of his encounter with the Man in Gray. In attempting to relate his experience exactly as it had happened, the ashen-faced employee haltingly described the mysterious visitor— the clothes that he wore, the look on his face, and the chair he had been sitting on.

With their curiosity aroused, and their bravery augmented by numbers, several members of the crew decided to venture into the ballroom as a group. After entering the elaborate hall and assuring themselves it was void of visitors, the workers approached the area where the ghost had been seen. Upon inspecting the table, and the long line of neatly placed chairs, the workers began to feel a bit uneasy when they discovered that every chair was in its place except for the one the Man in Gray had reportedly been sitting on. This chair had been moved, as if someone had pushed it away from the table before making his (or its) exit from the room.

Aside from the ballroom, other areas within Herrmann Hall are also said to be the sites of peculiar happenings. To take one example, some rather unnerving events have been reported in the building's main kitchen. Among them is the strange story of a large bread-tray cart that either was given a mighty push by a mischievous ghost or else suddenly developed an uncontrollable urge to travel on its own. According to a witness of the event, the cart (which was mounted on wheels and stood over four feet high) was parked in its customary spot in the kitchen, when, for no apparent reason, it shot across the room and crashed into a stove! A quick check of the area turned up nary a clue as to who, or what, had given the cart a push.

Still another location where odd happenings have been reported at Herrmann Hall is an antique elevator near the main entrance. Instead of moving from floor to floor at the mere push of an outside button, the old-style elevator could only be operated from within by hand. Given its design, several Postgraduate School workers are said to shake their heads in bewilderment over the elevator's unpredictable—and unexplainable—tendency to sometimes operate on its own and move from floor to floor without anyone at its controls!

The preceding stories only scratch the surface of strange happenings at the former Hotel Del Monte. Anyone who takes a serious interest in the subject will find it easy to collect additional accounts, such as those that tell of a waitress who was tapped on the shoulder by an "unseen thing"; a busboy who claimed a handful of glasses suddenly shattered in his hand; dental technicians who said they saw a ghostly image in an upstairs hall near the clinic; lights that have a habit of blinking on and off; doors that mysteriously open and close; and, last but not least, a strange and lonely figure that frequents the tower on certain dark and fog-filled nights. And that doesn't even take into account the many other reported appearances of the Man in Gray. As the stories continue to be told, the old Del Monte will surely maintain its place of honor as one of the Monterey Peninsula's most "haunting" sites.

The teenagers stood dumbfounded . . .

Perhaps the oldest, as well as the loveliest, of all of Monterey's historic structures is the Royal Presidio Chapel (also known as San Carlos Cathedral). Built in the 1790s, this Peninsula landmark has seen history come and go, and has served the people of the Monterey Bay area, as no other building has.

Over the years several strange and unexplainable happenings have been reported at the venerable church, not the least of which are accounts of a brightly burning candle that moves from place to place within the sanctuary, as if being guided by an invisible hand. An event such as this, witnessed by a single person, usually doesn't make believers out of many, but the following incident—witnessed by a group of teenagers—has caused more than one person to revise his or her thinking about the possibility of ghostly occurrences at the historic house of worship.

At one time the campus of Junipero Memorial High School practically adjoined the Royal Presidio Chapel (the site is now occupied by an elementary school). Late one night, a group of students were in the inner quad of the school. As the group sat huddled together, enjoying one another's company, the stillness of the night was suddenly shattered by the ringing of church bells. Shaken by the noise, members of the group glanced around the quad and then dashed toward the bell tower of the church. Upon reaching the tower, the teenagers stood dumbfounded, as the peal of the bells continued to echo through the night, even though not a soul could be seen pulling the ropes! A thorough search of the area failed to turn up any pranksters. All that could be found was a single lit candle in the deserted church.

With the message now being very clear . . .

To the west of the Royal Presidio Chapel is its old rectory (a residence for priests). Today the former rectory houses offices, storage facilities, and a small gift shop, together with the memory of a number of spooky happenings that are said to have taken place there.

Among the ghostly reports connected with the rectory are the somewhat common accounts of curtains mysteriously moving, footsteps being heard, rocking chairs rocking, stairs creaking, and assorted unidentifiable rattling sounds being made—all, of course, when no one was around to account for them. While at least a few of the mysterious happenings may be nothing more than figments of the imagination, the fact that stories continue to crop up leads one to believe that there must be some truth to at least some of the accounts.

One of the tales that has come to my attention is the story of a lady who was hard at work in one of the building's offices when she experienced the unmistakable feeling of a hand being placed on her shoulder. As you might expect, no one (at least no one *visible*) was present who could have touched her. From

She experienced the unmistakable feeling of a hand being placed on her shoulder . . .

that moment on, the shaken lady—who is well known in the church community—became convinced that the old rectory was frequented by at least one lonely spirit.

A second event that is associated with one of the building's offices happened a few years ago. The incident involved an employee of Junipero Memorial High School who had an office in the old rectory. Returning from a school outing late one night, he decided to do some paperwork in his office. After settling down and becoming engrossed in his work, the man was suddenly startled by the switching off of his desk light. Having felt uneasy about entering the darkened building in the first place, he immediately turned the light back on and thought seriously about leaving. Upon convincing himself there was nothing to be concerned about, he again settled down to work, only to have his desk light switched off for the second time. With the message now being very clear to him, the man hurriedly gathered his things and exited the facility.

An invisible something held him by the leg . . .

Our next account takes us to a Monterey building that is practically within a stone's throw of the Royal Presidio Chapel and its old rectory. The incident I am about to relate took place in the late 1960s, and involves a couple who had just arrived on the Monterey Peninsula and were looking for a room, or small apartment, they could rent. Finding "just the place" in an aged building near the Royal Presidio Chapel, the man and his wife proceeded to move their things in.

It was while they were moving their bed up a flight of stairs that the couple experienced the first of the strange happenings that would make them think twice about their dream dwelling. As the husband related to a friend later, an odd, "almost clammy" feeling came over him, making him feel as though he wasn't really there but instead had been "temporarily removed from the situation." As the feeling gradually passed, he tried to put it out of his mind, and he and his wife continued to move their things in.

That night, exhausted by the activities of the day, the couple had little trouble falling asleep. All was quiet until about 3:00 a.m., when the husband awoke with a start as an "invisible something" held him by the leg and began pulling him out of bed! As he tried to fight off the unseen thing, his efforts awoke his wife, who grabbed him by the arm, attempting to keep him from being dragged from the bed. With the invisible force now pulling both of them from the bed, the frantic wife let go of her husband, only to watch him being dragged across the room and toward the window. Upon reaching the window the unseen force stopped as suddenly as it had started, leaving the terrified man on the floor.

Confused, and extremely scared, the couple telephoned a friend and begged him to come over. Arriving as quickly as he could, the friend spent the remainder of the night with the frightened couple. Unable to explain what had happened, and terribly upset by the experience, the shaken pair spent the next day moving their things out of their home of only one night.

The interior of the house was a shambles . . .

From old Monterey, with its antique adobes and Spanish-style gardens, we now head toward Cannery Row and the part of town called "new Monterey." After rounding Presidio Curve—where many an accident has reportedly been caused due to a ghostly figure in the road—we continue on to the glitter and glamour of what was once the Sardine Capital of the World. Today "the Row," as locals often refer to it, is a pleasant hodgepodge of new businesses housed in the shells of old canneries. Nostalgic in appearance, particularly as seen from the sea, Cannery Row's canneries are, in their own special way, ghosts of a bygone era.

Another ghost from the same era once occupied a house only a short distance from the water. Although the house predates the days when the Row was alive with workers, whistles, and the smell of fish, the ghostly happenings recorded in this Monterey dwelling had their beginnings during the heyday of the sardine.

The story, as it was told to me, had its beginning in the 1930s, shortly before the man of the house died. Sensing his time was near, the man made a few last requests, among them being an expressed desire that his wife not work.

All went well until the canneries began operating on double shifts and an urgent call went out for workers. Being but a few minutes' walk from this booming industry, and having time on her hands, the wife decided to give the canneries a try. Carefully locking her house each day as she left for work, the lady returned at the end of her shift to find the house still securely locked, but the interior a shambles! Day after day this repeated itself, and night after night the tired lady would spend her time putting the house back in order. Finally, frustrated by what was happening, and exhausted from her continual cleaning, the lady quit her job—and from that time on her house remained as neat as a pin.

Many years later, the same lady reportedly experienced another occurrence in the house. On occasion, when the widow's grandson came for a visit, the young boy would be placed in an adjoining room, where he could sleep without being disturbed. Upon checking the boy to be sure everything was in order, his grandmother often observed a "luminous fog" hovering over him, as if guarding the lad and offering its protection.

Occasionally the ghost will roam through the house . . .

Bordering Monterey is the small city of Pacific Grove. Famous for its butterflies, and for being the last community in California to sanction the sale of alcoholic beverages, Pacific Grove is also noted for its many churches and for the attractive Victorian houses that are sprinkled about the town. Harbored in many of these turn-of-the-century homes, it is said, are a multitude of ghosts.

In one such house, described as being one of Pacific Grove's oldest, reports tell of a ghostly spirit that lives in an upstairs room. Apparently friendly in nature, and not the least bit of trouble, the ghost has long ago been accepted by the family that occupies the house. Occasionally the ghost will leave his upstairs room and roam through the house, making his presence known in a variety of subtle ways. Calling him George, for lack of a better name, the family members are said to get along well with their supernatural friend. Guests do sometimes remark how "spooky" they feel when they walk into George's room, and the presence of a cold spot on the staircase (traditionally a spot where spirits enter or exit a building) may discomfit some, but the family seems perfectly content to share the grand old house with George on an equal basis.

Once a day the house shakes and shudders . . .

Lining the waterfront are a number of Pacific Grove's oldest and most picturesque homes. It is in one of these older dwellings that a strange occurrence takes place. According to the owners, as well as numerous visitors, once a day—but at varying times—the house shakes and shudders. The owners have accepted the mysterious movement as part of the house's unique personality and happily report that they have become so accustomed to the shaking that they hardly notice it anymore.

A man is said to have died in one of the bathrooms . . .

Approximately one block from the water is an old Victorian home that once belonged to a prominent Pacific Grove family. Still standing on a corner lot, where its occupants command a view of the bay, the turreted structure remains a dignified land-mark of old Pacific Grove.

Assorted tales have been told about the elegant old house, but perhaps the one that provokes the most interest among ghost buffs is the story of a man who is said to have died in one of the bathrooms. For many years after the man's death, strange happenings are reported to have taken place in the room. Perhaps the strangest of all was the periodic flushing of the old-fashioned toilet. When plumbers were called to inspect the fixture, they, too, were mystified by its strange behavior. After repeated attempts to stop the flushing, the plumbers had to admit that the toilet's peculiar habits were caused by some-thing other than faulty plumbing.

One can sometimes still hear the panicky cries . . .

The history of Pacific Grove is as varied as that of any Penin-sula community. Even though it began as a Methodist retreat in the 1870s, a multitude of faiths and nationalities have shared in its rich heritage.

Among the ethnic groups that played a role in the Grove's early years were the Chinese. Numbering in the hundreds, these pioneer Peninsulans settled in the Point Cabrillo area and started a fishing village that became known up and down the coast. (Point Cabrillo is shown on some maps as Mussel Point. Stanford University's Hopkins Marine Station now occupies this site. The Chinese community is thought to have begun in the 1850s.)

One well-known resident of this bayside settlement was a man by the name of Chin Yen. Yen was said to be a master fish-erman, but he may have even been better known for his skill in collecting abalone. (An abalone is a type of shellfish with an oval shell lined with mother-of-pearl.) The meat of the abalone was highly prized by the Chinese, while the beautiful shells were equally prized by visitors to the Monterey Peninsula.

As was his custom, early one morning during an extra-low tide, Yen was climbing among the rocks in search of abalone. Having filled his basket, and noting that the tide was starting to come in, Yen wisely decided to head for home. Awkwardly carrying his cumbersome cargo toward the village, Yen rounded a huge rock and saw something that made his heart skip a beat. At the base of the rock was one of the largest abalone he had ever seen. Knowing what a price this prize would bring on the market, Yen decided he must have it.

Taking his trusty pry bar from his basket, Yen placed the bar between the unsuspecting abalone and the rock and gave it a quick wrench. Thinking he had loosened the suction-like hold of the abalone, and worried about the rapidly approaching water, Yen dropped the bar and placed his fingers under the abalone's shell, fully expecting to be able to yank the creature from the rock. Instead, he felt the abalone's strong grip pulling the shell down around his fingers. Too late, Yen realized the terrible predicament he was in. Try as he might, he couldn't free his fingers from the creature's vise-like grip, making it impossible for him to escape the rising tide. With the tide bringing the water ever closer, it was not long before the onrushing waves drowned Yen's screams and helped the abalone win its battle for survival.

Whether or not this tragic tale is true has been debated for many years. However, it is of interest to note that there are those who claim Yen's body was found at the next low tide, still held captive by the abalone. They say the body was taken back to the village, where much incense was burned, and where Yen was ceremoniously buried with a high iron fence surrounding his grave.

Just for the record, there are also those who say that, among the rocks along a certain section of the Pacific Grove shore, one can sometimes still hear the panicky cries of Chin Yen as

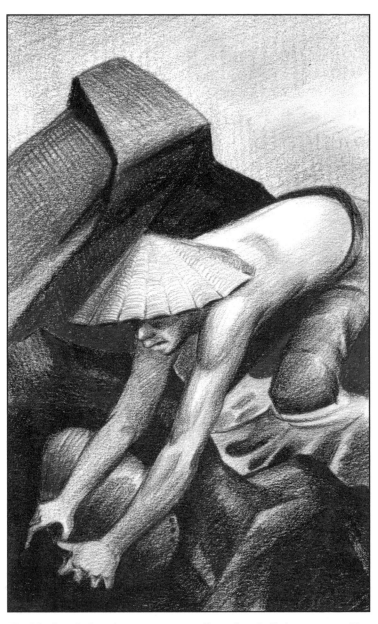

He felt the abalone's strong grip pulling the shell down around his fingers . . .

24

he begs for help in his long-lost battle to free himself from the death grip of his prize abalone.

With her unseen helper always leading the way . . .

A second tale connected with Pacific Grove's picturesque shoreline involves an even earlier group of Peninsula residents—local Indians. According to reliable sources, many years ago—perhaps around 1900—the wife of one of the Grove's early church pastors was in the habit of searching for Indian arrowheads as she took her daily walks on the beach. Frequently going on arrowhead hunts in the company of others, she repeatedly found more of the small artifacts than anyone else in the group, and it wasn't long before she became the proud owner of one of the area's most extensive collections.

One day, while on an outing with a friend, the pastor's wife mentioned her uncanny luck in finding arrowheads. The friend, who had a strong interest in spiritualism, answered by saying that it wasn't luck that helped the lady find her aged treasures, but, instead, it was the guidance of an Indian maiden who always walked with her.

Not nearly the believer in spiritualism that her friend was, the pastor's wife shrugged off the comment and continued to credit luck for her finds. However, soon afterward an event took place that made her reevaluate her thinking. One day, she was walking on the beach alone and not having the least bit of luck finding arrowheads. After spending considerable time in a fruitless search, the pastor's wife—half in jest and half in frustration—decided to ask the Indian maiden for help. Upon asking for guidance, she glanced at the sand and was amazed to find a beautiful and almost perfectly shaped arrowhead!

From that time on the pastor's wife reported that whenever she went searching for arrowheads she asked for help from the Indian maiden. With her unseen helper always leading the way, she continued to be one of the area's leading arrowhead collectors.

The sounds of the mighty black stallion can still be heard . . .

Before we leave Pacific Grove behind, a short tale of a ghostly black stallion may be of interest. As the story goes, parts of old Pacific Grove were thickly covered by a dense growth of Monterey Pine (as can still be seen in outlying areas). This forested section of the Grove is described as having harbored a number of lost souls along with an assortment of wild creatures.

One lost soul in particular has been remembered better than most because the search for her is said to have never ceased. According to the sad tale, a lovely young lass once became lost in the densest part of the forest. Upon hearing that his sweetheart could not be found, a heartbroken Pacific Grove lad rode off in search of her on a magnificent black stallion. As he frantically searched for his lost love, the forest echoed with the thundering sounds of his mighty black steed crashing through the trees.

Unable to find his sweetheart, the youth is said to have never given up his search. To this day, the legend states, if one listens carefully, the sounds of the mighty black stallion can still be heard as it crashes through the forested fringes of old Pacific Grove.

Muffled voices speaking as if their owners were in pain . . .

To the south of Pacific Grove are the private holdings of the Del Monte Properties Company. Known far and wide as Pebble

Beach, this picturesque area is renowned for its Monterey Pine forest, its Seventeen Mile Drive, its elegant inns, its beautiful—and challenging—golf courses, its scenic shoreline, its wind-sculptured cypress trees, and the numerous exotic villas that dot its landscape.

Less well known, perhaps, are the tales of mysterious happenings in the elegant mansions that are scattered throughout the forest and overlook the shore.* Several of these stories concern an imposing Spanish-style villa that once perched high on a hill overlooking Carmel Bay and distant Point Lobos. (The house has since been torn down.) Among the items that set the house apart were its striking red tile roof and its two elevators. Many years ago the stately structure was said to have been owned by an eccentric old lady who was also an invalid (which explains the elevators). After the woman died, the building remained vacant for a number of years. During this time locals began to look upon the house as a place where peculiar things happened, including the reported sounds of the elevators moving from floor to floor in the unoccupied edifice.

As is often the case with buildings that are said to be haunted, eventually somebody came along who tried to prove his bravery by spending a night within the structure. In this case, the somebody was a teenaged boy of the 1970s who was bet a considerable sum of money that he wouldn't be able to spend the entire night in the building. Accepting the bet, the boy bravely made his way into the villa while his friends waited outside, and settled down for what he hoped would be a profitable night's sleep.

---

*A number of incidents associated with the Pebble Beach area—such as accounts of the mysterious "Lady in Lace" who haunts the area near the Seventeen Mile Drive's famous Ghost Tree—are related in my book *Ghosts, Bandits and Legends of Old Monterey, Carmel, and Surrounding Areas.*

Except for a few moans and groans, things were comparatively quiet until about 1:00 a.m., when the boy began to feel and see "hot, humid clouds" even though the night was cool and the house was without heat or electricity. The clouds—coupled with a number of strange noises and the sounds of muffled voices speaking as if their owners "were in pain and barely able to talk"—began to take their toll on the shaken lad. Finally, after hearing an upstairs door slam shut, the boy decided he had had enough. He quickly exited the spooky structure, only too happy to trade the money he had hoped to win for the safety of his own bed.

The astonished teens made a gruesome discovery . . .

Only a few miles from the site of Pebble Beach's haunted Spanish villa is the beautiful and historic Mission San Carlos Borroméo del Río Carmelo, known to most simply as Carmel Mission. Recognized as the hub of Spanish California's Mission Trail, the mission was originally established in Monterey in 1770 and was moved to its current location the following year. Father Junípero Serra, the founder of the mission chain, chose Carmel Mission as his home, and it was here that he was buried after his death on August 28, 1784. His successor, Padre Fermin Lasuén, replaced the original adobe church with a stone structure that in time provided the basis for the restored building we see today. The handsome sanctuary and its surrounding grounds are looked upon by many as the most beautiful, and best preserved, of all of California's twenty-one missions.

Inasmuch as the church dates back to the late 1700s and has weathered countless crises over the years, it seems only natural that it would share in the Monterey Peninsula's history of ghostly happenings. One tale that comes to mind is similar to the preceding Pebble Beach account in that it involves a young lad who was bent on proving his bravery.

As the rather sad story begins, many years ago (most agree it was sometime in the 1870s) certain young men of the Monterey area were in the habit of proving their bravery by spending an hour in the dead of night in the mission confines. (At that time the sanctuary had not been restored, and much of it was in ruins.) As old-timers explained, young men performed this ritual in an effort to prove they were worthy of being accepted into the group.

One such lad marched into the fog-shrouded darkness of the crumbling church determined to outlast any of his predecessors. In this way he hoped to prove he was as brave as the best of them and was truly worthy of their acceptance. After keeping watch for a number of hours, his companions agreed that their friend had more than proved his bravery and was ready to become "one of the gang." There was only one problem—the fearless initiate was nowhere to be found!

After repeated, but fruitless, attempts to locate their companion and congratulate him on his acceptance, the somewhat disgruntled teenagers agreed that their friend must have outwitted them and had long since slipped out of the church and headed for home. It was not until the sun crept over the eastern hills that they learned that the intrepid lad had never returned home! Returning to the church to search for him, the astonished teens made a gruesome discovery. The lifeless body of the fearless boy who had so willingly ventured into the darkened church the night before was hanging by his own scarf from a rusty spike that had long ago been driven into a mission timber.

As the story concludes, old-timers maintained that the unfortunate youth had died of a heart attack. It was surmised that, as he wandered through the ruins in the dark, his scarf had somehow become entangled on the spike. As the terrified teen attempted to escape the clutches of whatever was holding him,

The lifeless body of the fearless boy was hanging by his own scarf from a rusty spike that had long ago been driven into a mission timber . . .

his heart faltered due to shock and fear. And for many years after this unfortunate incident, people in the vicinity of the mission spoke in hushed tones of seeing the ghostly figure of a lonely lad, complete with scarf, wandering through the crumbling ruins of the old stone church.

Pinned to the wall was the lifeless body of their friend . . .

A second tale involving Carmel Mission shares some morbid similarities with the one I have just related. As background to this story, you should know that many mysterious happenings reportedly took place on a trail that once connected Monterey and the site of the old Spanish mission. Long and winding, and passing through dense pine forests, the trail led over the summit of what is now called Carmel Hill. Along the way it passed through an area known to pioneer residents as the Devil's Elbow. Numerous early residents, in an effort to ward off evil spirits as they made their way over the fog-shrouded summit, placed a cross of twigs or tules by the trail as they began their journey. For this reason the route eventually became known as the Avenue of Crosses.

The beliefs of the old folks about mysterious happenings on the trail figure in our story, as many years ago a group of Monterey's daring young lads apparently were making fun of these superstitions. Things came to a climax when, in a bit of braggadocio, one of the boys stated he wouldn't be afraid to walk the trail alone at midnight.

Immediately taking their friend up on his boast, his companions decided he should make the walk that very evening. As proof that he had actually made the journey, they agreed that he should take a specially marked nail with him and drive it into the mission wall.

That night at twelve o'clock the group met at the Monterey entrance of the trail. After being given the marked nail, the

31

young lad wrapped his cloak about him, bade farewell to his friends, and bravely headed into the darkness.

Early the next morning his friends again gathered at the entrance of the trail. After following the Avenue of Crosses over the summit, they wound their way down the Carmel side of the hill to the mission. Upon reaching the church, they found more than they had bargained for. Pinned to the mission wall was the lifeless body of their friend, with the marked nail driven through his cloak and into the adobe!

What had killed the boy, and why his cloak was pinned to the wall, the legend doesn't say. It has been suggested that in his haste to leave the confines of the church the lad had accidentally driven the nail through a corner of his cloak and, as in the preceding story, not knowing what held him captive, had lost his life due to shock and fear.

As for me, given the similarities between this and the previous tale, I can't help but wonder whether the two somehow became intertwined over the years. Whatever the case may be, it's safe to say that both accounts are enduring parts of the legends and lore of the Monterey Peninsula.

His spirit would rise from the grave . . .

Known throughout the world to students of history and religion, Father Junípero Serra is considered the driving force behind Alta California's famed mission chain. As has been the case with many famous figures of history, the spirit of Father Serra is said to have returned to the scene of his labors after death had taken him from his people and his work. In the case of the good padre, the scene was none other than his Carmel Mission headquarters, where he was buried.

One such story about Father Serra's restless spirit apparently relates to the following statement found in an aged document: "Padre Serra, when near death, blessed California, and promised, if [his] life were spared long enough, to celebrate one hundred masses, that his blessing might remain on the land." As the legend has it, the dedicated missionary died before he was able to fulfill his promise. As a result, at midnight on the eve of each San Carlos Day (an annual church celebration and festival), his spirit would rise from the grave and he would celebrate a mass.

Just in case any current ghost seekers are intrigued by this tale, I should note that considerably more than one hundred years have passed since Serra's death in 1784. With this in mind, there seems little reason to stage a "ghost watch" at the site of the good padre's grave in Carmel Mission come future San Carlos Day celebrations.

"They were *goats,* not *ghosts!*"

As with Monterey's Royal Presidio Chapel, over the years several tales have been told about how the bells atop Carmel Mission's old bell tower sometimes ring in the dead of night. Perhaps, as is surmised by some, on special occasions the bells are rung by the ghostly spirits of lost souls or pioneer residents. However, even though this may be the case at times, there is a definite explanation for at least one bell-ringing incident.

A number of years ago I asked the long-time curator of Carmel Mission, the late Harry Downie, if it was true that ghosts once invaded the mission belfry and rang the bells. Upon hearing my query, he immediately set the record straight by saying emphatically, "They were *goats,* not *ghosts!*"

As Harry's rather comical story went, in Carmel's early days—long before the mission was hemmed in by houses—goats were kept in an adjoining field. One night, in their never-ending search for food (as well as adventure), the goats slipped through the barbed-wire fence that surrounded the field and proceeded to explore the mission. It was not long before the inquisitive creatures climbed the steep steps that led to the belfry and proceeded to munch on the bells' ropes. With each nibble the goats rang a bell, soon arousing the slumbering inhabitants of the nearby village. As the story concludes, until the truth became known there were those who were said to have been quite shaken by the "terribly troubled spirits" who so erratically rang the mission's bells!*

His two sons became insane and killed each other . . .

Our final Carmel Mission tale takes us to the period following the U.S. takeover of California in 1846. By this time, many of the old Spanish missions—including Serra's beloved headquarters—had long since fallen into a sad state of disrepair. It was during this period of neglect and decay that legend tells of an American farmer who acquired the land next to the Carmel church. Having no regard for the consecrated ground that bordered the sanctuary, the farmer is said to have plowed right up to the building's crumbling adobe walls, in the process disturbing the aged cemetery. Not overly concerned when his plow turned up the bones of several long-dead Indians, he went right on plowing.

Unbeknownst to the greedy gringo, the more he desecrated the cemetery land, the more misfortune he brought upon himself. The first indication that things were not right was when harvest time came and his fields were barren. From there, things quickly went from bad to worse. Before the second planting season arrived, the farmer's wife died. To add to his despair, while planting the ground near the church, his two sons became in-

_____

*Internationally known for his mission restoration work, Harry Downie was also a recognized authority on the life of Father Serra. After he passed away in 1980, he was buried on the grounds of Carmel Mission.

Not overly concerned when his plow turned up the bones of several long-dead Indians, he went right on plowing . . .

sane and killed each other. As if these events weren't tragic enough, the farmer's daughter is reported to have run off with a man who abused her, only to die before the next harvest season.

When the second harvest season came and went without any crops to show for his labors, the repentant farmer decided to let the sacred ground be. From that time on, the legend states, his luck changed and he received no more punishment for his "wanton desecration of the tombs of San Carlos."

To this day no one knows who the lady was . . .

Nestled in a forest of pine between Carmel Mission and nearby Pebble Beach is the picturesque village of Carmel-by-the-Sea. This quaint waterfront community is widely known for the eye-catching architecture of its residences (which range from fairy-tale cottages to elegant edifices overlooking Carmel Bay), its beautiful (and dog-friendly) beach, its unique collection of fascinating shops, its inviting art galleries, its gourmet restaurants, and its history as a refuge for creative folk (the famous poet George Sterling and author Mary Austin, to name two, were among its early settlers).

Also worthy of note is the village's interesting collection of ghostly tales, several of which center on one of my favorite Carmel buildings—an aged two-story structure located right in the heart of town. The building I have in mind was built by a popular pioneer resident in the 1920s and was occupied by him for a number of years. Many of the ghostly happenings that are said to take place in the structure were typical of the things he did when he was alive, a fact that has led numerous Carmelites to conclude that the odd occurrences are nothing more than the ramblings of the late owner as he continues to putter about the place.

Described by some as "the village's first packrat," and known to many as a poet, playwright, producer, and business-man, this colorful Carmel character was also known to have had a considerable collection of antiquated things. Among them were a great many books. He was very proud of these publications and wanted them close at hand. For this reason he was in the habit of moving them from room to room, often clapping them together in the process to rid them of dust. As you might guess, the movement of books, and the sounds of volumes being clapped together, were among the happenings that were experienced in the upstairs portion of the building long after the owner passed away.

Other reports tell of the ghostly but identifiable sounds of the immortal Jack London in conversation with the building's owner. (London was one of George Sterling's best friends, and he was an occasional visitor to Carmel.) Equally strange was the way the building's lights had a habit of going off at the most inopportune times, a fact that created both concern and frustration over the years. However, the situation was resolved when it was learned that the lights could be "talked back on" with a few kind words, as if a ghostly hand controlled the switch.

Perhaps the oddest occurrence at the structure is reported to have taken place during the month of December. For many years a popular shop was located in a portion of the upstairs floor. Catering to visitors and residents alike, the shop did a remarkable Christmas business, and its owner was in the habit of hiring extra help for the holiday season. For several years in a row a local man filled in during the December rush. Each year this gentleman observed the ghostly figure of a woman seated on a stool behind one of the counters. Whenever the man glanced her way, the ghostly image would immediately turn away, as if she were extremely shy, or perhaps did not want to be recognized. To this day no one knows who the lady was, or why she was visible only to a single individual.

The ghostly figure of a "long-ago lady" . . .

Upon leaving Carmel and heading south on Highway One, we soon pass a beautiful castle-like building that overlooks a sandy white beach. Known as the Carmelite Monastery and completed in 1931, it was constructed to house a community of cloistered nuns who had moved to the area six years before. By the time Highway One was completed (circa 1937), the stately structure was already a coastal landmark.*

The highway lies approximately halfway between the monastery and the beach. It is on this scenic stretch of road that many accidents have narrowly been averted as motorists reported the evasive actions they were forced to take in order to avoid hitting the ghostly figure of a "long-ago lady" who was frequently seen crossing the road. Who the lady was, and where she was headed, are unanswered questions of this "monastery mystery."

A human skull stared at him through eyeless holes . . .

Almost bordering the grounds of the Carmelite Monastery is beautiful Point Lobos State Reserve. Referred to as "The Great-

---

*In case you are wondering about the coincidence of names, Carmel-by-the-Sea owes its name to a group of Carmelite friars who accompanied Spanish explorer Sebastian Vizcaíno to the shores of California in 1602. Vizcaíno allowed the missionaries to name the area around Carmel Bay in honor of their heavenly patron, Our Lady of Mt. Carmel. When cloistered nuns from the same religious order arrived to start their new community in 1925, they inherited the proud Carmelite heritage that had begun locally more than 300 years before. (Incidentally, Vizcaíno also was responsible for naming the bay and community of Monterey, though in that case the honored patron was a more earthly figure—the viceroy of New Spain, the Count of Monterey.)

est Meeting of Land and Water in the World," Punta de los Lobos Marinos (Point of the Sea Wolves) boasts a history of shipwrecks, smuggling, pirates, whaling, and lost treasures. Interestingly, local legend also states that the land once changed hands in a game of cards!

The Point Lobos story I'd like to share here dates back to the early 1900s, when the Whaler's Cove area of the rugged promontory was the headquarters of a small, Japanese-operated abalone canning industry. The tale revolves around a Japanese abalone diver who found what appeared to be the remains of an aged Spanish galleon. Forgetting all about abalone, the thrilled diver began poking around the long-lost wreck. Finding what seemed to be the barnacle-encrusted remains of a warrior's helmet, he excitedly brought it to the surface.

Upon examining the helmet, the eager treasure seeker carefully turned it over—only to let out a scream and drop it back into the sea! Recounting the story later, the shaken diver explained how he had looked into the helmet and found a human skull seemingly staring at him through eyeless holes as it greeted him with a grotesque grin!

Realizing something terrible had happened . . .

A second tale of a long-lost vessel off the rugged Point Lobos shore tells of a mysterious bell that tolled a death knell for an aged sea captain. As the story goes, around the turn of the century (1900) many seafaring folk heard the subdued sounds of a ship's bell as they plied the treacherous waters off the Point Lobos promontory. One well-known San Francisco-based captain—described as being "hard on his officers" and a "dried-up old fossil who lived like a recluse ashore and never left the bridge [of his ship] while at sea"—became obsessed by the tales of the bell. Locating its whereabouts became the number-one priority for the bewhiskered captain.

Agreeing that the sounds came from a submerged source—possibly from a long-ago wreck—the captain hired a Monterey-based diving crew led by a hard-hat diver from San Francisco. Captain and crew then set out with high hopes of finding the bell and the wreck from which it came.

After two days of searching and following the sounds of the bell, the diver found the remains of an aged ship. In short order he brought to the surface the barnacle-covered and worm-eaten nameboard of the vessel.

When the grizzled captain saw the nameboard, he became extremely excited and insisted that he be allowed to don the diving gear and visit the wreck. Because of the depth, and the dangers involved, the diver and crew attempted to discourage the old seaman from making the dive. But because he had hired the men and was paying for the trip, the captain had his way. He was soon fitted with a diving suit, given detailed instructions, and lowered from the launch.

A short time later the man in charge of the captain's air hose hollered for help as he saw the hose snaking to the surface, coiling and squirming from the pressure of the air. Realizing something terrible had happened, the rest of the crew frantically grabbed the lifeline and gave it a yank, only to have it, too, come to the surface unattached. Even more shocking, a quick inspection revealed that both of the lines had been deliberately cut, leaving the captain to die among the bones of the long-lost ship.

It wasn't until later, when all the facts became known, that the story of the captain's fascination with the ghostly bell, and the circumstances of his strange death, took on added meaning. According to the original source, it was discovered that the vessel from which the nameboard had come was the very ship the captain's wife had been traveling on more than thirty years before, when it mysteriously vanished on a voyage down the rugged California coast!

After two days of searching and following the sounds of the bell, the diver found the remains of an aged ship . . .

California's haunted Brigadoon . . .

Slightly south of Point Lobos is the coastal community of Carmel Highlands. Described by some as California's Brigadoon, this cliffside community is known for its elegant inns, scenic vistas, and seaside villas, as well as for having been called home by many prominent people, including the famed photographers Edward Weston and Ansel Adams.

With its background including everything from buccaneers to bootleggers, the Highlands boasts a colorful history. Also a part of its storied past are tales of ghostly happenings, a number of which are reported to have taken place in a magnificent mansion that overlooks the restless Pacific. Reportedly haunted by the ghost of a child, as well as the spirit of the wife of the original owner, this stately old structure is also said to boast a history of constantly being added to, like the famed Winchester Mystery House of San Jose, California. The "first lady" of each of these abodes is said to have believed that she would not die as long as she kept adding to the house. The amazing 160-room Winchester House is a famous example of what such a conviction can lead to, and the Highlands mansion bears out the same theme on a much smaller scale.

Among the lavishly appointed rooms of the Highlands home are seven bedrooms, each with its own fireplace (the largest of which is big enough for an adult to walk into). Detached from the main house is an elaborate library that, for many years, was kept locked with a large and ornate padlock. Many of the ghostly happenings associated with the mansion are said to have taken place in the library, including the distinct sounds of the estate's original mistress asking the butler "if she could leave."

Another occurrence that mystified more recent residents of the hillside house was the strange behavior of their German shepherd, which had a disconcerting habit of running through the mansion, occasionally stopping to bark at a variety of unseen things. However, the latest report from the home's most recent occupants is that the ghosts are "friendly." On that happy note, we can bid goodbye to California's haunted Brigadoon.

They could hear the bells of the lead horse . . .

Long before automobiles became commonplace, when the vision of a coastal highway was only a distant dream, a wagon trail led south of Carmel Highlands toward the primitive paradise of Big Sur. Winding through canyons and along rocky cliffs, the rugged trail was beautiful to look at—as long as one had nothing but time and the winter rains or summer fog hadn't set in—but torturous to travel.

Slightly south of the Highlands a small stream flows from the Santa Lucia Mountains and meets the Pacific in a mass of bubbly foam. According to old-timers, this mountain stream was aptly name Mal Paso (meaning "bad crossing") Creek. Those who were forced to travel the old coast road, it is said, often shook their heads in frustration as they told of being stranded in the muddy bottom of Bad Crossing Creek for as long as a day.

One aged account tells of a wagon driver who lost his life to the rugged terrain of this coastal wilderness. Hauling a load of tanbark (used in the tanning of hides) near Mal Paso Creek, the man approached a second canyon crossing that boasted a trail both steep and crooked. Looking toward the small stream at the base of the canyon, the man noticed that the wagon route followed the cut of an old trail along the canyon wall. Near the canyon floor the cliff-clinging road made a sharp turn as it continued to follow the twisting mountain stream.

Having reached the top of this steep trail, the man set the brakes on his wagon and checked his team. With everything in order he began the slow descent toward the creek below.

The bells on the collar of the lead horse jangled monotonously as the team slowly made its way down the trail. Suddenly, the wagon's brakes gave out, and the heavily loaded rig began picking up speed. Staying with the wagon and its cargo, the driver managed to keep his team on the road until they reached the sharp turn near the canyon's bottom. Going much too fast to round the curve, the frightened four-horse team—along with the wagon and its frantic occupant—went over the side and plunged to the creek below, strewing tanbark up and down the canyon floor.

The wagon and its frantic occupant went over the side and plunged to the creek below . . .

Unhappily, the tale concludes, the driver was killed in the fall. No mention is made of the fate of the horses, but the story does go on to say that "for a number of years after the accident people who used the canyon road at night swore they could hear the bells of the lead horse as they passed the spot where the wagon went over the side."

The ranch hand received two letters trimmed in black . . .

Just south of Mal Paso Creek and the canyon of the jingling bells is the vast acreage of an early coastal ranch. As coincidence has it, this historic property also boasts an interesting account of mysterious bells.

The incidents in this tale, which date back to about 1900, were shared with me by a man in his eighties (now deceased) who was a friend of the fellow who experienced them. This latter gentleman was a man of Portuguese descent who had only recently come to this country from his home in the Azores (a group of islands off the coast of Portugal). After arriving in California, he had taken a job as a ranch hand. Working a six-day week, the man was given Sunday off to do as he pleased.

Loving horses, and soon learning to love the Santa Lucia Mountains, the ranch hand was in the habit of taking long horseback rides into the rugged coastal mountains on his day off. Late one Sunday, after riding for hours in the Santa Lucias, he was heading back to the ranch when he came upon a small canyon with a stream flowing through it. Ready for a brief rest, and knowing his horse was thirsty, he let the horse drink while he lay in the tall grass watching the clouds drift in from the Pacific. It was while he was watching the clouds, feeling at peace with himself and his surroundings, that he heard the sounds of tolling church bells.

Surprised by the sounds, the man listened intently. He was even more surprised when he realized that the bells sounded exactly like those in his village church in the Azores. Understandably confused, the ranch hand mounted his horse and rode to the main ranch house, where he told his strange tale.

The owner of the ranch, as well as others who heard the story, were interested in the man's account, but found it hard to take it seriously. They were of the opinion that the ranch hand had become tired during his long ride and that, as he lay in the peaceful surroundings of the mountain canyon, he had drifted off to sleep and dreamed that he had heard the bells of his church in the Azores.

Convinced he had not been dreaming, and that the sounds were real, the ranch hand returned to the canyon at about the same time of day on the following Sunday. As he had done the week before, he let his horse drink while he lay down to rest, only to hear once again the distinctive sounds of the bells of his village church. Positive he wasn't dreaming, he jumped on his mount and raced to the ranch house, where he repeated his story.

Discussing the incidents more seriously on this second occasion, the owner and his family, together with the ranch hand's fellow workers, began to speculate about the sounds. Perhaps, they suggested, something had happened to a member of the man's family, and with no way to communicate with California, except by mail that would take weeks to travel by sea from the Azores, someone back home was trying to communicate with him through the ringing of the church bells.

The next Sunday, the ranch hand again visited the remote canyon, but to his relief, there were no church bells to be heard. After another week came and went without any sounds of bells tolling, the matter was gradually forgotten, and things went back to normal.

It wasn't until approximately six weeks after the first incident in the canyon that the matter again became very real to the people of the coast ranch. On that fateful day the ranch hand received two letters trimmed in black. Upon opening the letters he immediately realized the significance of the strange sounds he had heard. Exactly one week apart, on the very days he had listened to the mournful tolling of the bells, his mother and his father had died in his far-off village in the Azores!

They peered through the inky black of
Palo Colorado nights . . .

As old-timers continued down the old coast road, they soon came to a picturesque mountain canyon boasting giant redwood trees that seemed to reach to the heavens. Named by the Spanish, the area is still known as Palo Colorado Canyon. (Roughly translated, *palo colorado* means "red wood," "red stick," "red mast," etc.) Many years ago a small town was located on a flat near the canyon's entrance. The community, called Notley's Landing, took its name from the two brothers who operated a mill in the heart of the redwoods.

The industrious Notley brothers oversaw a small coastal lumber empire and kept many men busy felling trees, sawing lumber, and making such things as shakes, shingles, railroad ties, and posts. The timber, along with vast quantities of tanbark, was brought out of the canyon by cable, on the backs of mules, by sleds, and on heavy-duty lumber wagons. When the wood reached the mouth of the canyon, it was loaded on small freighters and lumber schooners that were anchored in the rocky harbor near the entrance of Palo Colorado Creek. When the lumber supply was finally exhausted, the town—along with what was frequently referred to as "the wildest dance hall on the south coast"—gradually disappeared.

As with other landings and secluded harbors up and down the coast, Notley's Landing didn't gain all its fame from its lumber industry. Other "enterprising industries" at the remote harbor reportedly included the smuggling of Chinese in the late 1800s. And yes, during the Prohibition era of the 1920s, the landing was said to be a favorite spot for rum-running. In more recent times, the canyon and its surrounding area have been in the news for still other reasons, not the least of which was the discovery of a wrecked World War II bomber (complete with an odd assortment of bones) that was found by two hikers on the remote slopes of a nearby Santa Lucia peak.

As for ghost stories connected with Palo Colorado Canyon, perhaps the most frequently told tale tells of a ghostly wagon and spirited team that in "nights of old" were often heard racing down the canyon. Pioneer residents who experienced the strange phenomenon told how they dove for cover as they heard the sounds of the free-running horses and wild-riding wagon charging down the narrow canyon road. Cowering in the bushes or behind nearby trees, the old-timers peered through the inky black of the Palo Colorado nights, hoping to catch a glimpse of the thundering steeds and the mysterious wagon. Each time the unmistakable sounds of pounding hooves and clattering wheels passed them by, without so much as a shadow to be seen or a track to be found.

Several people are said to have heard the baffling sounds of the unseen wagon and its free-running team. As for who owned the team, and whether there was a driver spurring the ghostly steeds on, no one has ever said. All that is known is that the invisible team and wagon were always headed west and that, wherever they were going, they were in a terrible hurry!

The black-clad figure vanished ...

The Santa Lucia Mountains of Monterey County are the most awesome of California's Pacific peaks. Used as markers by the earliest navigators, and proving formidable barriers to the first Spanish explorers, these rugged mountains are rich in history and romantic legends.

Among the more mysterious and ghostly of the Santa Lucia tales are the numerous accounts reported by long-ago settlers— as well as people of more recent times—that speak of strange "dark watchers" who frequent the mountain wilderness. The fact that the "watchers" have been described by many—including two of Monterey County's twentieth-century literary greats,

John Steinbeck and Robinson Jeffers—adds considerable credence to these oft-told tales.

Steinbeck, a Pulitzer- and Nobel-Prize-winning author, and Jeffers, a poet of international renown, both knew the Santa Lucias well, and both mentioned the dark watchers in their works. In Steinbeck's short story "Flight," a character sees "a black figure" on a barren spur and looks quickly away, "for it was one of the dark watchers." Steinbeck continues, "No one knew who the watchers were, nor where they lived, but it was better to ignore them and never to show interest in them." Even more mysteriously, Jeffers, in his poem "Such Counsels You Gave to Me," tells of "forms that look human to human eyes, but certainly are not human. They come from behind ridges and watch." These brief passages serve as proof that stories of "dark watching men" (or whatever they may be) have circulated throughout the Santa Lucias for many years.

With both Steinbeck's and Jeffers's works dating back to the 1930s, an account of more recent vintage will perhaps help to convince skeptics that Monterey County's dark watchers are more than just figments of old-timers' imaginations. The tale was told by a prominent Monterey Peninsula man who was the principal of a local high school. As the story goes, the principal and two companions were on a hunting trip in the rugged coastal mountains. After much hiking the principal became separated from his friends but was able to keep them in sight as they trudged along on a parallel ridge some distance away. As he continued up the ridge he was climbing, he frequently glanced at his companions, not wanting to lose them in the wilderness.

Suddenly, as the principal looked toward the other ridge, he noticed a strange, dark figure standing on an outcropping of rock. Remaining quiet, he studied the lonely figure. Later he described it as dressed all in black, including a hat and long coat or cape. He also told how the mysterious watcher stood very still as it surveyed the rugged mountain landscape. But when

49

Suddenly, as the principal looked toward the other ridge, he noticed a strange, dark figure standing on an outcropping of rock . . .

the principal shouted to his friends to turn around and look, the black-clad figure vanished!

With the figure disappearing from view, and with the questions of who it was, where it had come from, and why it was there, remaining—as always—unanswered, the only certainty is that the name of a respected principal can be added to the long list of people who have been bewildered by the mysterious dark watchers of the Santa Lucias.

The heartbroken lass jumped from the cliff . . .

In following California's Highway One down Monterey County's scenic south coast, motorists can't help but marvel at the massive Santa Lucia Mountains and the rugged Pacific shore. As they follow the twisting highway and cross numerous beautifully designed bridges, they will also pass Indian sites dating back thousands of years; a sacred "white" mountain called Pico Blanco, where local Indians believed humanity had its beginning; numerous shipwreck sites (the waters of Point Sur have often been referred to as a "Pacific graveyard"); giant redwood trees; castle-like homes, many of them designed and occupied by world-known personalities; historic landings, such as Partington Cove and its hand-carved tunnel; morbid Massacre Cave, where prospectors discovered the bones of ten long-dead people; long-lost treasure sites (Spanish gold coins are said to have been found near the south coast's Willow Creek); and, not least, the Los Burros Mining District, home of the famed Last Chance Mine, and producer of hundreds of thousands of dollars in gold.

Long before they pass into neighboring San Luis Obispo County, southbound travelers will also pass a steep and almost sheer cliff known to locals as Lover's Leap. As a long-time resident of the area explained to me, Lover's Leap is where a young lady took her own life decades ago. Jilted by her lover, the heartbroken lass is said to have jumped from the cliff on a cold, foggy night. As the tragic tale concludes, the mournful cries of the young lady as she fell from the cliff can still be heard on certain dark and fog-filled nights.

He had come to them through the air . . .

In a northeasterly direction and across the mountains from Lover's Leap is beautiful and historic Mission San Antonio. Founded in 1771, the mission was the third establishment in Father Junípero Serra's historic mission chain. Situated in a peaceful, oak-studded valley, it has often been described as the most tranquil of all the California missions.*

For those with an interest in the strange and unexplained, Mission San Antonio is especially notable for the many ghostly and spiritual tales that are connected with it. One of the oldest, and most interesting, of these accounts was related to the padres by an elderly Indian woman in the mission's early days. Said to be near the century mark in years, the woman came to the padres asking to be baptized. Asked why she desired baptism, she told a tale of long ago, one she said she had heard from her parents when she was a little girl.

As the tale went, long before Father Serra brought the cross to the Valley of the Oaks (as the area around the mission is often called), a man wearing clothing similar to Serra's had come to the Indians and had told them the same stories the mission padres were telling. It was the memory of her parent's tales, and the connection between those accounts and the current

---

*Today the mission grounds consist of an 85-acre preserve within the Fort Hunter Liggett Military Installation. Established in 1941 on 200,000 acres in south Monterey County, the fort was originally called the Hunter Liggett Military Reservation. It was named for General Hunter Liggett, a noted commander in World War I.

Said to be near the century mark in years, the woman came to the padres asking to be baptized.

teachings of the padres, that had prompted the woman to seek baptism.

When questioned further about this long-ago "bearer of the cross," the aged woman told how he had not come by horse, or by foot, but instead—on four different occasions—he had come through the air!

With their curiosity aroused, the padres asked other Indians whether they had heard similar tales. To their surprise, most of the Indians in the valley seemed to know of the flying father. In fact, the padres learned, the story was handed down from generation to generation as part of the teachings of the local Indians.

In carrying this remarkable tale a bit further, it is of interest to note that approximately 150 years before California's mission chain got its start, a tribe of Indians from the area we now know as New Mexico sent messengers to find missionaries who would come to their land and baptize them. When the padres reached this tribe, they were astonished to find that the Indians were already so well informed about the Christian way of life that they were ready for baptism!

Strange as it may seem, this New Mexico tale is accepted as fact by many historians. Stranger still, when records were traced in an effort to learn more about the missionary who had originally taught the tribe of Indians, a letter written by a nun in far-off Spain was uncovered. In this document the nun stated that she and others had made "spiritual visits" to the Indians of this area and had taught them the story of Christ. She described in detail not only events, but also places the "spiritual missionaries" had visited.

What make this more intriguing to some is the possibility of a connection between the New Mexico Indians and the people whom the padres encountered around Mission San Antonio. The San Antonio Indians, it has been said, resembled those of the New Mexico tribe in many ways. Examples of these similarities included their habit of using the traditional southwestern *manos* and *metates* (rubbing and grinding stones used in the preparation of food) rather than the mortars and pestles that were employed throughout much of California. Of even greater significance was the similarity of the languages spoken by the tribe in New Mexico and the small band of San Antonio Indians. Considering all of this, perhaps, as Father Francisco Palou indicated nearly two centuries ago, the Christian knowledge of the Indians in the Valley of the Oaks—and their eagerness and willingness to help the mission fathers—should be attributed to the supernatural powers of Spain's Sister Mary of Jesus de Agreda in sending missionaries to a distant land.

As you might expect, others prefer a more down-to-earth explanation for the knowledge of Christianity that was displayed by the San Antonio Indians. Whatever the case may be, the Indians of this tranquil California valley have presented historians with a puzzling mystery, one that remains unsolved to this day.

The headless horselady of San Antonio . . .

A second mystery connected with the Mission San Antonio area involves the strange tale of a headless horseback rider who has frequently been seen in the vicinity of the aged church. Referred to by many as "the headless horselady of San Antonio," this ghostly figure on her gallant mount has been observed by old-timers of the Jolon, Lockwood, and Mission San Antonio areas, as well as by soldiers at Fort Hunter Liggett (all of which are in close proximity to each other).

As far as I have been able to determine, the story of the headless horselady apparently had its beginning in the mid to late 1800s. Many of the accounts that mention the legend also say that at about this time there were groups of Indians still living in the vicinity of the decaying church and that prospectors were combing the nearby mountains and streams looking for gold. (The community of Jolon, founded around 1860, was a jumping-off place for many of the miners.) As you will see, these facts play an important role in the legend of the headless rider.

As the tale goes, one of the Indian women who lived in the San Antonio area was in the habit of slipping away from her husband and spending time with a prospector in the nearby hills. It was not long before the husband caught the two together. In a jealous rage he killed his wife and beheaded her with an axe! The enraged husband then buried the body in one grave and the decapitated head in another.

With this as the background, and with added information stating that many of the local Indians believed a body must be buried intact before it can lie at rest, it is certainly tempting to conclude that the headless horselady observed by so many is, in all probability, the unfaithful wife in an eternal search for her head!

It is certainly tempting to conclude that the headless horselady is, in all probability, the unfaithful wife in an eternal search for her head . . .

"There was nothing from here up . . ."

In days of old, long before the military occupied the area around Mission San Antonio, residents of nearby communities, as well as those who lived on ranches and farms in the valleys and hills of the easterly Santa Lucias, were aware of the legend of the headless horselady and her never-ending search for her decapitated head. Many of the old-timers, however, attributed the sightings to hallucinations the Indians experienced while they were under the influence of peyote powder. (Peyote powder was obtained from mescal cactuses. It is described as an intoxicating drug.) It was with this in mind that several local history buffs tried to discover whether there was any truth to the tale. The researchers made several attempts to talk to descendants of Indians who had lived and worked in the San Antonio area long ago. Unfortunately, the latter-day Indians preferred not to comment on the story.

With the descendants not wishing to discuss the tale, and with many of the old-timers being of the opinion that the mysterious sightings were nothing more than drug-induced visions, the story would probably have died a natural death if several new sightings hadn't been made in the 1960s and 1970s. In most cases, these more-recent sightings were credited to soldiers who had been standing duty at various lonely guard posts on Fort Hunter Liggett's vast acreage.

The majority of the happenings are described as having taken place in the very early hours of the morning in an area of the fort known as the ammo supply point (ASP). An account of one of these incidents, which dates back to 1974, describes the headless lady as riding on a horse along a nearby crest of mountains. Referring to the figure as Cleora, the bewildered soldier went on to say, "I saw it while at ASP in December. It was a female, I'm sure of that. And there was nothing from here up [pointing to his neck]."

In another ASP incident, a soldier was standing guard duty when he saw a headless figure approaching. With the figure disregarding his command to halt, the soldier drew his weapon, only to have the ghostly image vanish into the night.

A third happening involves a soldier who was on guard duty in a small shack near what is known as the Gabilan impact area. Upon hearing a knock on the door, he challenged the visitor but received no answer. Cautiously going out of the shack to see who was doing the knocking, the soldier could find no one and returned to the shack. It was after he was back inside and peering out of a window that he saw the headless figure of a lady wearing a cape (or overcoat) and long, flowing robes.

Additional accounts were shared with me by a man I will call Brother Anthony, who spent many years at Mission San Antonio. Brother Anthony was something of a student of history and was very interested in stories about the area. When accounts of the headless rider were brought up, he would nod knowingly and occasionally add a tale or two himself.

During one of our talks (in the mid 1970s) Brother Anthony said, "Over the years several people have reported seeing or hearing the headless horsewoman as she rides by the church." He also told of four MPs who came to him in 1975 swearing that they not only had seen the ghostly apparition but had chased her and her spirited mount with their jeeps, only to lose her as she disappeared into the wilderness.

The accounts could go on and on, but, as with many other stories of this kind, perhaps it is best to let the matter rest and let you decide for yourself how much truth there may be in the tantalizing tales of the headless horselady of San Antonio.

They were forced to stop short as the riderless horse galloped past them . . .

Before leaving the Valley of the Oaks, I'd like to share one more fascinating nugget from the treasure chest of Mission San Antonio tales. The account was told to Brother Anthony by a respected old-timer who swore it was true.

The story takes place in the late 1800s, when a small party of local residents went to the mission—which was then a collection of crumbling ruins—to have a picnic. After finding a suitable clearing amidst the high, dry grass some distance from the church, they settled down for an enjoyable outing.

The picnickers had just made themselves comfortable when they heard the sounds of an approaching horse. Standing to see who the visitor might be, they were surprised to see a lone cowboy ride up to the church, swinging his lasso. Not knowing who the rider was or what he was up to, the locals watched from a distance as the stranger proceeded to lasso the cross on the roof of the church. The cross was already leaning at a precarious angle, and it was obvious to the onlookers that it would not be able to withstand the pull of the rope for long. As the cowboy wound his end of the lasso around his saddle horn and began to back away, they ran toward the mission, shouting for the stranger to leave the cross alone.

As they ran through the high grass, the alarmed locals lost sight of the unwelcome visitor. Suddenly, however, they were forced to stop short as the cowboy's riderless horse galloped past them.

Confused as to what had happened, and concerned as to the fate of the rider, the picnickers searched the nearby area. They soon found the lifeless body of the cowboy in the brush. To this day the old-timers who are aware of this account are unable to explain how the cowboy died—but they do know that the cross he had attempted to pull down remains secure in its place high atop the roof of Mission San Antonio.

The Mission of Sorrow . . .

In leaving Mission San Antonio and following the eastern foothills of the Santa Lucia Mountains north toward the Monterey Peninsula, we eventually come to a second mission site, known to historians as Mission Nuestra Señora Dolorosísima de la Soledad. Named for "Our Most Sorrowful Lady of Solitude," the mission was established to minister to the Indians of the Salinas Valley.

Inasmuch as the Soledad mission counted a high of 688 converts in 1805, it can justifiably be said that it fulfilled its role as a major link in the mission chain, but when the minuses are stacked against the pluses, the outpost stands out as one of California's least fortunate churches. In fact, it is rather ironic that this solitary sanctuary is number thirteen in California's long line of missions, as lady luck seems to have stacked the deck against the remote valley church from the beginning.

From its very inception, when the church goods and furnishings failed to arrive on the scheduled boat, Mission Soledad's fate was a matter of some doubt. Not only did the searing heat of the Salinas Valley summers, and the damp, windy cold of the winters, take their toll, but some of the early padres who were placed at the mission proved to be unsuitable choices for their duties as pastors to the local Indians.

Add to these challenges a litany of woes that includes severe summer droughts, an epidemic that almost wiped out the entire population, a disastrous fire and attack by hostile Indians, an earthquake that almost destroyed the church, numerous floods that did considerable damage, confusion and disharmony prompted by nearby soldiers, and the mysterious murder of three Indians, and it is not difficult to understand why the Soledad church has been referred to as the Mission of Sorrow. Yet somehow the mission managed to survive despite this multitude of problems, not to mention a dwindling number of Indian converts.

In its later years Mission Soledad was blessed with some outstanding padres, not the least of whom was Father Vincente Francisco de la Sarría. The Salinas Valley mission became home to this man of God in 1828, and it was here that he remained until his death seven years later. With only his beloved Indians as company in his final years, this remarkable man unselfishly gave himself to the few remaining converts who were still willing to call Mission Soledad home.

According to tradition, Father Sarría was saying mass one Sunday morning when his strength gave out and he died in the arms of the people to whom he had dedicated the last part of his life. Grief-stricken by the passing of their friend and father, the Indians are said to have carried his body over the long, lonely trail to distant Mission San Antonio, where their beloved padre could receive a proper Christian burial.

She would slit the throat of her slumbering guest . . .

With the preceding account serving as an introduction to the Soledad area, we proceed to a couple of tales that revolve around the historic Los Coches Adobe, located slightly south of Soledad on Highway 101. In days of old this aged structure served as a stage stop for travelers. During the heyday of California's great gold rush, and on into the 1860s, many miners who had struck it rich (as well as those who headed home nearly broke) stopped at the wayside inn for a meal and, if pennies permitted, a round of cheer. Occasionally a weary traveler would choose to forego the "comforts" of a bumpy ride on the evening stage and spend the night.

As the first of our tales relates, little did these long-ago travelers suspect that their decision to remain at the inn might be the last decision they would ever make. Tradition states that the hefty and somewhat "mannish" miss who presided over this Salinas Valley stop would wait until all was quiet, and then, with knife in hand, stealthily sneak into a wayfarer's room, slit the throat of her slumbering guest, and steal his gold!

In disposing of the body the stage-stop murderess would then carry the corpse to an old, unused well and deposit it at the bottom of the shaft. The well has long since been covered over, and old-timers wonder whether the stolen gold might also be "covered over" in a neatly dug hole somewhere on the property.

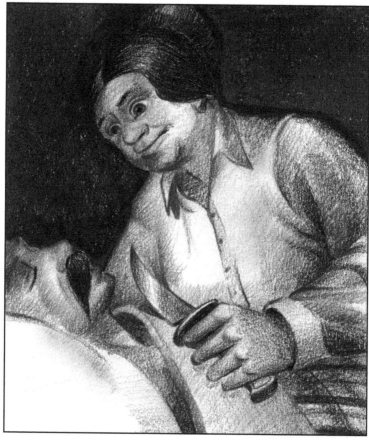

Tradition states that the hefty and somewhat "mannish" miss would wait until all was quiet, and then slit the throat of her slumbering guest . . .

As strange as it seems . . .

As indicated in the last section, this brief account also concerns the historic Los Coches Adobe. The incident was recorded by a small group of Salinas Valley photographers who had gathered at the site. After looking at several of the pictures they had taken of the interior of the building, the camera buffs reported a number of objects and "unseen things" that appeared in the pictures, but that were not visible to the naked eye.

Among the more interesting of the items that had mysteriously appeared was the distinct pattern of aged wallpaper that had been affixed to the structure's walls sometime in the distant past. As strange as it seems, the wallpaper pattern does not appear to the human eye except when it is captured on film.

Perhaps, at some future time, the "magic eye" of someone's camera will reveal to its owner the cache of gold that, as described in the preceding section, the stage-stop murderess is believed by some to have buried near the historic inn . . .

The heavy metal plates strike the walls with frightening force . . .

With our short "circle tour" of south Monterey County leading us back to the Monterey Peninsula, a trip through the upper reaches of Carmel Valley will allow me to recount a tale or two of ghostly happenings pertaining to this area.

Upon leaving Los Coches and heading toward the Peninsula via Carmel Valley, one passes the turnoff to Paraiso Springs (which boasts a colorful history of its own, including tales of ghosts) and eventually arrives in the Arroyo Seco section of the upper valley. According to reports from the occupants of an old schoolhouse in this outlying area, several mystifying events have occurred in the building, almost making them think that the ghost of an aged schoolmarm is chastising her "pupils" (the building's inhabitants) for their misconduct.

Without doubt the most mysterious—and certainly the scariest (in terms of potential bodily harm)—of the many happenings that take place at the site is the unnerving habit of the heavy steel lids atop the wood-burning stove that, upon occasion, fly from their customary places and strike the walls with frightening force!

More than one old-timer claims she was an Indian princess . . .

In continuing toward the Monterey Peninsula on the winding Carmel Valley road, one will eventually come to an area known as the Cachagua. Reminiscent of scenes of the old west, the Cachagua has its own unique history, including tales of lost mines, buried treasure, and, yes, a scattering of homes that are said to be haunted.

One of the best known of these houses is a structure that stands near the eastern entrance of the Cachagua. Built in the late 1800s, this historic dwelling has, over the years, been the scene of several ghostly happenings. Perhaps the most common of these occurrences is the sighting of a "mystery lady"—dressed in a long, flowing white gown—climbing the outside staircase at the rear of the building. Even though no one seems to know the origin of the story, more than one Cachagua old-timer claims she was an "Indian princess."

A second example of the kind of ghostly accounts associated with the house tells of a couple and their pet dog who, on a number of occasions, were visited by an unseen thing. According to both the husband and his wife, the visits most often occurred on peaceful nights when they were in the living room enjoying the comfort of a cozy fire. Suddenly, they related, the dog—as if in a trance—would wake from a deep sleep and stare toward the opposite side of the room. With the hair on its back raised, and its nose quivering, it would whimper and whine as it continued to stare at the opposite wall.

Upon looking in the direction their aroused pet was staring, the bewildered couple couldn't see a thing out of place; nor

Perhaps the most common of these occurrences is the sighting of a "mystery lady"—dressed in a long, flowing white gown—climbing the outside staircase at the rear of the building . . .

could they sense an additional presence in the room. However, upon checking the area that seemed to distress the dog, the couple detected an unmistakable cold spot, even though the room was warm due to the briskly burning fire. (A cold spot, as previously discussed, is where spirits are said to enter or exit a building.)

As to who their mysterious visitor was, and why the invisible presence repeatedly returned to the site, the house's occupants don't know. Upon reflection, however, they both agree that—whoever it may be—their unknown guest does add an interesting dimension to the already colorful history of this aged Carmel Valley home.

The mournful sounds of someone crying in the dead of night . . .

As we leave the Cachagua behind and follow the Carmel Valley road back to the Monterey Peninsula, our journey approaches its end. Before bringing this book to a close, however, I'd like to take a brief detour and swing by the bayside community of Marina. Bordering former Fort Ord (which has its own history of ghosts, and which is now home to California State University, Monterey Bay), Marina prides itself on being the "Gateway to the Monterey Peninsula." Many long-time Peninsulans, however, remember the community best for its small-town atmosphere (which is now a thing of the past) and its beautiful begonia gardens.

The mysterious happenings I wish to discuss take place in a dwelling that is relatively new compared to most of the other haunted houses described in this text, having been constructed sometime around the 1950s. Nevertheless, the happenings are classic examples of the kinds of "supernatural shenanigans" that are reported in other so-called haunted houses of much greater age on the Peninsula and elsewhere.

Among these events are reports of eerie feelings and sensations experienced in certain parts of the dwelling, unexplainable noises and scary sounds, and interior walls that shudder and shake in the middle of the night. Less typical, perhaps, are the mournful sounds of someone crying in the dead of night. Even though the sounds are very distinct, and have been heard by several people, no one has been able to find a trace of anyone (or anything) that could account for the distressing cries.

Another rather unnerving incident at this location was experienced by a house guest who had retired for the night. Suddenly, as she was about to drift into slumberland, she felt an almost unbearable "dead weight" on her legs and chest. With considerable effort she managed to get out of bed and reach the door. Upon exiting the bedroom and reporting the incident to the owner, the frightened lady vowed never to sleep in "that room" again!

People have debated for years what causes these odd occurrences in a relatively recent dwelling that doesn't have a long history of tragedy, death, or despair. In bringing this tale to a conclusion, however, I should mention that the owner of the house began to take the incidents more seriously when he was told his home had been built on, or near, an ancient Indian burial ground . . .

Afterword

As I mentioned in the Author's Note at the start of this book, the first edition of this work followed the publication of *Ghosts, Bandits and Legends of Old Monterey, Carmel and Surrounding Areas,* my first book-length foray into local lore. Since then, I have written seven other books about ghosts and mysterious happenings. In some of these publications I have "returned to the scene of the crime" and borrowed a bit from my first two ghost offerings, but only with the idea of expanding the original tales. Quite often, after one of my books or articles is printed, someone will contact me with additional information, or I will learn more about the subject through other sources, such as aged diaries, letters, scrapbooks, and newspapers, and, perhaps most important of all, my interviews of old-timers. Before I know it, it's time for a new book or two!

Among my later ghost books are ones that delve more deeply into such subjects as the Custom House, the Stokes Adobe, the Hotel Del Monte, the Royal Presidio Chapel and its old rectory, Carmel Mission, and Monterey County's magnificent south coast. The area from Point Lobos south, in particular, has a book all to itself, called *Ghosts of the Big Sur Coast,* which even includes an account about fabulous Hearst Castle. Haunted happenings throughout the Golden State are the subject of a longer work entitled *California Ghost Notes.*

Those who have become intrigued by Monterey's old adobes may want to check out a more recent publication called *Ghosts and Mystery Along Old Monterey's Path of History.* This work not only includes a great deal of factual information about many of the aged adobes and other points of interest in California's first capital city, but also delves into the numerous ghost stories associated with so many of old Monterey's historic structures. And for those who are young at heart, or who are interested in the world-renowned writer Robert Louis Stevenson (who stayed in Monterey circa 1879), I've written a book for young readers (in the ten to twelve age group) called *The Strange Case of the Ghosts of the Robert Louis Stevenson House.*

Tales of the supernatural, as plentiful as they are, are only part of the rich lore associated with Monterey and its surrounding areas. I've also written books of local interest about such things as shipwrecks, sea monsters, gold mines, treasures, bandits, and pirates. So, if you enjoyed this work, and would like to learn more about the magical Monterey Peninsula and the spectacular coastline of central California, see the list of books on page 73.

Now that the commercial is over, I would like to thank you for your interest. And, since you've made it this far, I'd guess you have more than just a passing interest in ghosts. With this in mind let me add that if you have any stories that you'd like to share (particularly those dealing with the Monterey Peninsula or other parts of California), I'd love to hear from you. You can write me in care of Ghost Town Publications, P.O. Drawer 5998, Carmel, California 93921, or send an email to info@ghosttownpub.com.

In the meantime, track down the old-timers in your community and listen to their tales, visit your local library and read about the spooky places and mysterious happenings in your town, and keep your eyes and ears open for interesting accounts about the strange and unexplained. Who knows, maybe there are enough stories waiting to be uncovered for you to write your own book about things that go bump in the night!

Good luck, and happy haunting . . .

Acknowledgments

As with most publications that touch on history, many sources were needed to document this work. Among printed sources, I am indebted to the following: *Calle de Alvarado,* by Antoinette Gay; *Flight,* by John Steinbeck; *A Piney Paradise,* by Lucy Neely McLane; *Sea Bells,* by John Fleming Wilson; and *Such Counsels You Gave to Me,* by Robinson Jeffers.

The following newspapers and weekly guides also added immeasurably to many of the stories: *King City Rustler; Monterey Peninsula Herald; Monterey Peninsula Review; Monterey Trader;* and *Seaside Post.*

Although these publications were invaluable in the research for this work, I obtained some of the most interesting information from the diaries and memories of private individuals, many of whom trace their Monterey County roots back several generations. With this in mind, it perhaps goes without saying that much of the information contained herein has never been published before. And it is to the contributors of these "ghostly tales and mysterious happenings," as well as to all those who collect their stories, that this book is dedicated.

It would be extremely difficult to list all of the other people who, at various points along the way, have helped create this work. However, I would be remiss indeed if I did not acknowledge at least a chosen few. For this reason I would like to thank the following for their help, interest, and encouragement, and, of course, for the many stories they have shared: Jeri Barone, Ryan Cooper, Mike Curtis, Harry Downie (of Carmel Mission), Fred Houston, Max Plapp, Dorothy Ronald, Jessie Sandholdt, Mary Sherman, Troy Tuggle, Joe Victorine, and "Brother Anthony" (of Mission San Antonio).

I also extend a hearty thank you to my editor, John Bergez, and my two artist friends, Ed Greco and Tony Hrusa, for their interest and involvement.

As a closing tribute, I want to thank my wife, Debbie; my son, Erick; and our English bulldog, Joshua Jonas McCabe, for their support and understanding during the many trials and tribulations I encountered in writing this book.

Books by Randall A. Reinstedt

Regional History and Lore Series
Bringing the colorful history of California's Central Coast to life for adults and older children

California Ghost Notes
Ghost Notes
Ghostly Tales and Mysterious Happenings of Old Monterey
 . . . and Beyond
Ghosts, Bandits and Legends of Old Monterey
Ghosts and Mystery Along Old Monterey's Path of History
Ghosts of the Big Sur Coast
Incredible Ghosts of Old Monterey's Hotel Del Monte
Monterey's Mother Lode
Mysterious Sea Monsters of California's Central Coast
Shipwrecks and Sea Monsters of California's Central Coast
Tales, Treasures and Pirates of Old Monterey
Where Have All the Sardines Gone?

History & Happenings of California Series
Putting the story *back in hi*story *for young readers*

Lean John, California's Horseback Hero
One-Eyed Charley, the California Whip
Otters, Octopuses, and Odd Creatures of the Deep
Stagecoach Santa
The Strange Case of the Ghosts of the
 Robert Louis Stevenson House
Tales and Treasures of California's Missions
Tales and Treasures of California's Ranchos
Tales and Treasures of the California Gold Rush

Ghost Town Publications
P.O. Drawer 5998 ◆ Carmel, CA 93921 ◆ (831) 373-2885
www.ghosttownpub.com